About the Publisher

4Fun Publishing, a member of **BLVNP Incorporated**, 340 S. Lemon #6200, Walnut CA 91789, info@blvnp.com / legal@blvnp.com
NOTE: Due to the highly emotional reaction of some people to works of erotic fiction, any email sent to the above address that contains foul language or religious references is automatically deleted by our anti-spam software and will not be seen. All other communications are welcome.

DISCLAIMER

Please don't be stupid and kill yourself. This book is a work of FICTION. Do not try any new sexual practice that you find in this book. It is fiction and not to be confused with reality. Neither the author nor the publisher or its associates assume any responsibility for any loss, injury, death or legal consequences resulting from acting on the contents in this book. Every character in this book is over 18 years of age. The author's opinions are not to be construed as the opinions of the publisher. The material in this book is for entertainment purposes ONLY. Enjoy.

JACK RYDER

THE CHEATING GAME

NAUGHTY EROTICA

The Cheating Game
Naughty Erotica

By: Jack Ryder

© **Jack Ryder 2015**
ISBN: 978-1-68030-307-0

Chapter 1

I can't really remember exactly how I came up with the idea. The WHY is as clear as day, even after all these years. The entire motivation behind my sly little plan was driven by a deep rage fueled lust to get even with a malicious infidelity and to fulfill a childhood fantasy. I had fantasized about my sexy MILF mother-in-law ever since I started dating her daughter way back in high school. I had been leery of my best friend Peter's lust for my wife almost nearly as long. It would ultimately be those two things thrown together by circumstance that would drive me to make the plan and take the actions that I have.

But I am getting way ahead of myself here. I should start at the beginning, so you may understand why this happened and maybe you won't hate me in the end. It's not like I ruined anyone's life or physically hurt anyone. Although I manipulated some situations, I did not force anyone to do the things they did all by themselves willingly. Although I started some wheels in motion, the results found a momentum of their own. The bottom line is that cheaters cheat and I took full advantage of that.

I would have to say that the event that started the ball rolling happened the night of my bachelor party. It wasn't a surprise to anyone that Nikki and I were going to tie the knot. We have been inseparable since we first met on the first day of high school. My best friend Pete has been the only other significant person that has been part of the last three years of our lives, along with Nikki's mom Krysta.

Nikki and I wanted to get married right after graduation, so we would have some time together before she travelled across the state to attend college. We knew the distance would keep us apart for certain amounts of time, but we were both determined to continue our plans so we could build a successful life together. I would stay home and continue working, so I could take over my father's company someday. Nikki would complete her education and someday become my accountant. We had a plan and we were certain that we could make it work.

Pete insisted on throwing a big bachelor party. It was sort of embarrassing that most of the fellows that attended that night were really Pete's friends. Although I knew most of the fellows, they were just mostly acquaintances from various school functions. I had asked Pete to keep the party a low-key event, but he went all out anyway. It was my initial feeling that Pete just wanted to seem like a big shot to all his other buddies. It wouldn't be till some time later, that he had an entirely different motive.

It was really your average rented bar sort of bachelor party. Complete with strippers, lap dancers, and a lot of liquor consumption. I was pleased that he had at least thought ahead enough to contact a shuttle bus taxi service to get everyone home safely. I made it a point to not get nearly as drunk as the rest of the fellows. But it seemed like Pete was trying his best to force more drinks on my way even if I left them untouched.

Throughout the evening, each of the strippers made their way over to kiss and rub their mostly nude bodies all over the groom to be. It was very unsettling to me as the fellows took cell phone photos each time they did it. But I didn't make a big deal about it, since they were taking photos of all the girls rubbing all over the other fellows as well. I did notice that Pete seemed to get quite excited each time he took photos of the girls humping on me. He seemed to have a huge grin as he snapped his shots. Just before midnight, shortly after I told Pete I was about ready to go home, one of the strippers pushed me down onto my chair and proceeded to sit on my lap for a lap dance.

The fellows were all whooping and hollering, as she ripped off her top and shoved her big hooters in my face. When I saw the flashes from Pete's camera, I knew how this could look if Nikki ever saw them. As I grasped her hips to lift her off, her unfastened bikini bottom fell off and Pete snapped a photo with her nude body pressed against mine.

After I shoved the girl off of me and told her to get lost, I grabbed Pete by the collar and demanded that he delete all those photos. At that moment I was closer to punching my best friend than I could ever recall. I was livid that he had not only allowed this to happen, but he had greedily photographed the whole thing. He slowly deleted each of the photos while I sat there and watched. What I did not know at that time was that he had already forwarded them to his laptop at home.

On the drive home in the rented shuttle, Pete apologized for his actions. He insisted that he would never send those photos to Nikki because he loved her too and would never want to hurt her in any way. What I missed that evening from that apology, was that he said he LOVED HER and he did not say he was sorry that he had already hurt me. He didn't say that he understood how much those photos could affect my life or damage MY relationship. You don't really think of those sorts of things when you're 19 years old on the way home from a bachelor party.

<<O>>

The second red flag occurred the next day. It was Saturday morning and I received a call from Krysta.

She needed some assistance to pick up the flowers for tomorrows wedding and asked if I could come by with my van to help her with that. I was a bit hung over, but it wasn't bad since I had kept a handle on my drinking last night. I told her that I would be happy to help in any way that I could.

Two things happened that day. One of those stuck in my mind and germinated in my fantasies from that day forward. The other one would come back to haunt me several years later. I was amazed when Krystal climbed into my van that morning. Her long blond hair was pulled back into a ponytail. I have always thought she looks especially sexy when she wears it that way. But it was the way she was dressed that made my jaw fall open.

Krysta was wearing an extremely short and tight pair of those micro-fiber shorts that were stretched so tight that they were practically transparent. As she sat down on the seat, I could see the camel toe between her legs. The very loose tank top she had on rested so low on her 36CC breasts that I could nearly see her nipples. She had the bottom twisted just underneath her tits and tied in a knot on her right side. "Thought it would be nice to be comfortable," she giggled when she saw my jaw hanging.

On the way to pick up the flower arrangements from the florist, Krysta told me that she had something terrible to tell me. I instantly wondered what she could possibly tell me that would be terrible. She reached into her purse and pulled out a large envelope that had obviously been opened. "This was taped to the front door this morning," she announced very softly. "It is a letter to Nikki from Pete," she added.

I was fortunate that I was setting at a red light when she told me that or I probably would have slammed on the brakes and caused an accident. "Maybe you should pull over into a parking lot," Krysta suggested as I stared at the envelope well past when the light turned green. I quickly cleared the traffic on my right and pulled into a convince store parking lot. It was one of those with a large parking area because they also sell fuel and need room for large trucks. I pulled to the back of the lot behind the truckers.

In the letter, Pete professed his love to Nikki. He informed her that he has felt this way since the day we all met three years ago. He said he couldn't live with himself if he didn't at least tell her before she made the mistake of marrying me. The next part of the letter said that he had photos of me with other women. He said he had proof of a naked woman rubbing herself all over me. He insinuated that this had happened many times in the past.

My hands were trembling with rage, as I finally turned to read the second page. Pete advised Nikki that she should not marry me because I have had the hots for her mother since the day we first started. He claimed that I had told him that day that I would rather bang her mother anytime anywhere. He then went on to claim that I have repeatedly told him over the years how I spied on her mom in the shower and bragged about all the times I stole her panties and masturbated on them.

The rest of the letter described little physical attributes that Krysta has. A mole on her left breast. A birthmark on her right thigh just inches from her pussy. The little white triangles on her tits and trunk from her bikini tan line. These are all things a normal teenage boy would notice about a gorgeous woman in a bikini. But Pete made it sound like I had seen her naked.

I was vibrating so violently that it felt like a thousand volts of AC electricity was coursing through my body. It was rage and humiliation flowing back and forth in opposite directions. I was so stunned that I didn't notice that Krysta reached over to turn off the ignition. I did not notice her pry the letter out of my fingers. I did not notice that I was screaming and tears were rolling down my cheeks.

"We better get in the back till you calm down," she whispered as she pulled me between the seats into the back of the van. "We don't need any nosey people prying into your business," she added as she closed the curtains to block any view from the front windshield. Krysta just held me in her arms and rocked me gently for quite some time while I just cried and vibrated. "It's okay baby, she never saw it," she whispered softly. "She will never see it."

When I finally began to calm down and the vibrating subsided, Krysta gently pulled me down till we were lying on our side facing each other. "I know that every word of that was written by a selfish, jealous, and lovesick young man," Krysta told me. "I know that you would never cheat on Nikki and I know that everything he described about me could be seen by anyone who saw me in a bikini," she added.

I could feel her breasts mashed against my chest as she hugged me a bit tighter. I felt her soft warm lips against my neck as she continued to talk. "Was any of it true... about me?" she whispered. I felt a shiver in my stomach as her lips brushed my neck. It felt like she kissed me gently. "It's okay if you did... have a crush on me," she whispered. This time I was certain that I felt her kiss me. "I have had those same feelings for several years," she whispered. "But I never acted on them just like you didn't." For the next several moments Krystal held me tenderly and softly kissed the side of my neck

Chapter 2

Krysta had a funny sort of expression on her face as she suddenly sat up. I watched with amazement as her hand slowly reached down and pulled her loose tank top off over her head. "I want you to see me,

Zack," She whispered hoarsely. "Pete tried to seduce me too, but you are the only one I want." My dick swelled to full erection as she shimmied out of her tight little shorts. "I want you to see all of me," she told me as she removed her thong panties.

My dick was so hard that it was pressing straight out against the soft fabric of my sweatpants. "Do you think I'm pretty, Zack?" Krysta asked softly as she gazed into my eyes. "Oh Yes, Krysta. I have always thought that you are pretty... always," I gasped my reply. My body was again vibrating, but this time it wasn't rage. It was pure lustful arousal.

"Would you like to touch me, Zack? It wouldn't really be cheating... since you're not married yet." I knew deep in my heart that it was wrong. But the consuming lust within happily agreed with that rationale. "I have always wanted to touch you, Krysta. As long as I can remember." My hands were already moving up to fondle her huge 34DD globes. "Oh my God, they are beautiful," I groaned as her nipples became erect against my fingers.

"Yesssss, Zack... Yessssss!" I felt Krysta's body shudder as I raised my head to suck on one nipple while I gently pinched on the other. The musky scent of her arousal was intoxicating and filled the inside of my van. "You can touch... my other place," she moaned as I felt her hand slipping into my sweatpants to grasp my throbbing prick.

I could feel my dick oozing fluid onto the back of her hand as I shoved my hand between her bare legs and started rubbing my fingers up and down her slippery wet gash. I was amazed by how aroused I was.

Nikki and I had done this countless times in the past. I had never felt this aroused before. I had never gotten this hard.

"Are you sure this is okay?" I moaned as her hand gently rubbed my dick. "Yessss, baby, it's ooh-kaaay," she purred. Krysta reached down with her free hand and pushed my hand forcefully so my fingers rammed into her drenched sexhole. "Yes, Zack... Yessss," she groaned. I felt some more precum ooze into her hand as she began to jerk me off.

Krysta began gently kissing the side of my neck as we masturbated one another for the next couple of minutes. "This may be the only chance we get... to do what we both have wanted," she whispered in my ear as she sucked on my earlobe. "Let's take this one chance... to have it," she told me as she pushed me onto my back and swung her legs over me to straddle me.

"Gaaawwwd, I've wanted you," Krysta moaned as she guided my dick into her drenched gash. "Oooooh, Krysssssta," I gasped my reply as her hot slick pussy engulfed my prick. "Oh god, you're huge," Krysta panted as my 3 inch girth stretched her inside. The tip of my 9 inch dick was wedged against her cervix as she became completely impaled on my rigidness.

"Are you sure this is okay?" I moaned. But my hands were already mashing on both of her tits as she began to rock back and forth. "This is better than okay... this is spectacular," she grunted her answer.

Krysta was now my very first lover since Nikki had insisted that we wait till after marriage to have intercourse. "Fuck me Zack, Fuck me," she moaned in a very deep throaty voice. The sensation of her hot vagina pressed around my cock was the most intense and wonderful sensation I had ever felt. "You are my first, Krysta," I moaned my reply.

As if spurred on by my confession, Krysta began slamming down harder and faster. Her eyes seemed like they were rolled back into her head as her fingernails pressed into the skin on my chest. "So precious, baby... so precious," she moaned. Without meaning to, my dick began to erupt inside of Krysta's saucy vagina. "Ooooh no! I'm sorry... I'm sorry," I gasped as my dick ejaculated again and again.

When Krysta felt the warmth of my semen flooding into her womb, her body suddenly jerked and began to convulse. Because I had never had sex with anyone, I was afraid at first that I had hurt her somehow.

"Ooooh, Zack. It's so good, s-o-o-o-o good," Krystal moaned in that deep husky tone again. My dick erupted one last time.

"There's nothing to be sorry about, Hun," she laughed as she fell forward to kiss my lips. "That was fantastic for your first time ever," she whispered it in my ear. "It takes practice to learn how to hold on longer," she giggled playfully. "I'd be happy to let you practice anytime you want." My cock swelled back to full erection as she kissed my neck and nibbled on my ear. I flipped Krystal onto her back and fucked her a second time. This time, I lasted almost ten minutes. This time, I shoved my dick as far into her pussy as I could reach as I unloaded three more wads of semen into her belly.

We were both panting for air when I rolled off of her. "I will never forget this, Zack," Krysta cooed softly as she rolled back into my arms. We laid there together in the back of my van for quite some time afterward. It felt so delicious to feel her soft naked body against mine that I never wanted to let go. We gently petted each other while we giggled and chatted. Then, it fell silent for several minutes.

"There's something else I should tell you," Krysta mumbled as she glanced up into my eyes. I could see a concerned sadness in her eyes as her hand came up to brush some hair away from my face. "I saw Pete sneaking out of Nikki's bedroom window the night we had her 18th birthday party." Krysta's voice was sort of strained and trembling. "I don't know how long he was there or what they were doing... but it seemed wrong since that was the night you announced your engagement. Especially since it was 2am in the morning when I saw him leaving."

I could feel a knot growing in my stomach as she kissed my neck and told me she was sorry to have to tell me all of this. "It happened again on prom night." This time her voice sort of sounded like the words wanted to stick in her throat. "I was still awake when you brought Nikki home at midnight and then left several minutes later. I heard a funny noise about 3am and again saw Pete climbing out her window like before."

There was a very long silence while I let that all sink in. "I'm so very sorry, Zack." Krysta finally broke the silence. "That is why... I will never regret this," she whispered as she gently kissed my cheek. It's amazing how intensely aroused a person can become when they are enraged. "I will never regret this either," I growled as I rolled her over and shoved my rigid prick into her cum filled slit. "Taaaaake me, Zack. Take me," Krysta moaned.

This time, I rutted into her for nearly twenty minutes. This time, Krysta wrapped her legs around my waist and bucked wildly to match my brutal thrusts. Our grunts and moans sounded like two animals mating as if there were no tomorrow. When I climaxed, my dick exploded so forcefully that I felt like I blew the head of my dick off inside of her. Krysta flopped and convulsed beneath me for quite some time before her body finally went limp. "Wow... that was fuckin... amazing," she panted.

It was a quiet drive back to Krysta's house after we delivered the flowers to the local lodge where the wedding was scheduled. We were both lost in our own thoughts as we made the drive across the city.

"Are you still going to go through with it?" She finally asked softly. "That will be up to Nikki," I told her as we turned onto the street that led to her house. "I will give her a chance to decide if she wants to back out or not." Krysta reached over and touched my hand as we pulled into her driveway. "Regardless of what happens. This will always be the best day of my life," she whispered.

Nikki was standing in the living room when we came into the house. "It is bad luck to see the bride the day before the wedding," she gasped loudly. "If you don't talk to me right now, there will be no wedding," I growled my reply. I could see the stunned look on her face as she glanced at her mother and then back to me. "I'll just... go upstairs now," Krysta announced softly.

"Pete will not be coming to the wedding... if there is one," I announced tersely. I could see the shock wash across her face. "Oh... is that a problem?" I goaded her as I stepped forward so I was face to face.

"But... he's your best friend..." Before she could complete her sentence, the rage welled up inside and I shouted at her. "HE'S NOT MY FUCKING FRIEND. HE'S TRYING TO STEAL MY GIRL AND HE TRIED TO MAKE IT LOOK LIKE I FUCKED THE STRIPPER GIRLS THAT HE HIRED FOR THE BACHELOR PARTY." I screamed it so loud that I was certain that Krysta heard it all the way upstairs.

Nikki was stunned into silence. The expression on her face was that of fear and surprise and uncertainty. Although I calmed my voice, my anger was still obvious as I told her about the letter Pete left on the door. "He professed his love for you, he begged you not to marry me," I growled as I leaned forward to be even closer to her face. "He accused me of wanting to bang your mother and tried to frame me with those fucking hookers he hired for the party." My voice raised a bit with that.

I stepped back and folded my arms. "Is there something you need to tell me now?" I asked softly. "Have you changed your mind about marrying me? Do you think Pete might be a better choice?" I stepped back another step and waited for her answer. The expressions that ran across her face changed so quickly that she would have looked like a rainbow if she had been a camellia. "No... I... Ugh... no."

I saw her knees buckle slightly and she quickly lowered herself onto the loveseat just behind her. "Pete has always been fun... but you are the one I want to marry." Her voice was faint and scratchy. "You are the one that I can build a nice life with. You are the one that I want to be with," she whispered so softly that I could barely hear it.

When you're not quite twenty yet, you don't notice that she did not say that she was in love with me. She did not say that she had been faithful to me. She did not say that she wanted to be mine forsaking all others. Those sort of ideas and understandings come much later. Usually after having experienced the absence of those qualities in the relationship.

Chapter 3

It was a small wedding at the local Elks Lodge attended only by family and close friends. There weren't many friends on my side of the ledger, but mom's large family made up that disparity. Since Pete would not be there to be the ring bearer, I simply had my father do the honors. He was thrilled with the small task. "I should have had you do the bachelor party too," I teased him. We all could have been home in bed by 9pm and I could have avoided the shit storm that Pete created.

After I called Pete to tell him he was no longer my friend and was not welcome at the wedding, he made it a point to send all of the party photos to twitter and tumbler and several other sites. I made it very clear to him that he should stay away from Nikki and he was not to contact either of us ever again. I told him he was dead in our lives from here on out.

The ceremony took place late in the afternoon so that the reception in the main ballroom would take place right at dinner time. Since there were only two dozen people to feed, we had arranged a prime rib dinner with baked potatoes, salads, and various types of bread rolls. I'm not really sure what brand the red table wine was but it went very well with the meal. We all decided that champagne would not be necessary.

The cake cutting ceremony went fairly smoothly. I playfully stuck a dollop of the creamy icing on Nikki's nose. She, in-turn, shoved half her slice of cake in my mouth, making a mess all over my goatee. When Nikki's Dad took the first dance with the bride, I took the opportunity to pull Krysta into my arms as well.

"This must be our dance," I told her as I guided her out onto the floor.

Although it was too risky for us to let our hands wander, Krysta pressed her breasts against my chest and rested her head on my shoulder. "I wish you were inside me right now," she whispered in my ear. "I wish we were back in my van," I whispered back. Krysta giggled softly as she gently rubbed her tits back and forth against my chest. "You've made my panties wet," she said softly. "You gave me a boner," I told her in response.

As soon as the song was over, I pulled Nikki into my arms. "Now it's the groom's turn," I announced as I pulled her against me to conceal my erection to everyone watching. "God, you're hard," Nikki gasped when she felt the erection pressed against her belly. "I can't help it," I whispered. "You look so pretty in that wedding gown." I squeezed her ass while I said it. "And I can't wait to strip it off you so we can finally make a woman out of you." I added playfully.

I noticed that Nikki had an odd look on her face as we left the dance floor. At the time, I figured that she was probably just nervous about losing her virginity. "I'll be gentle with you," I whispered as I held the chair for her to sit down. "I will go very slow." Nikki did not respond to the statement. The look in her eyes seemed like she was far away at that moment.

<<O>>

I pulled Nikki into my arms as soon as we were in the honeymoon suite and kissed her passionately. "I have waited for this for so long," I whispered as I began to slowly unbutton all the tiny buttons on the back of her wedding gown. Nikki glanced up at me and she had a sad look in her eyes. It seemed like she was struggling for words.

"There's something I need to tell you," she informed me sheepishly. "I'm not exactly a virgin anymore," she told me so quietly that I could barely hear her. "What does that mean?" I asked as I stepped back to see her face better. "Either you are a virgin... or you're not," I pointed out. "I accidently... lost my cherry," she told me as her eyes fell to stare at the floor. I was incredulous now! "How on Earth does one do that?" I groused.

"On my birthday... I accidently let... ugh... got carried away... with my... favorite dildo," she told me. I could hear a tremble in her voice. At that exact moment, I remembered what Krysta had seen on the night of Nikki's birthday. I could envision Pete climbing out of her bedroom window. I felt a shiver run up my spine. "Was your favorite dildo named Pete?" I growled as I stepped further away. "Geezus, Nikki. Why did you marry me?" I shouted. "You should have married him."

Before Nikki could answer me, I grabbed my car keys and left the room. I was relieved that I didn't see anyone from the wedding party as I made my way to the parking garage. Once I got into my van, I really had no clue where to go or what to do. I just sat there for quite some time with my keys in my hand, staring out the front window at the blinking marquis sign just outside. VACANCY... VACANCY... VACANCY.

The ring tone of my cell phone startled me since my mind was a million miles out of nowhere. "Please come back to the room," Nikki sobbed softly. "I waited for this night for a long time too," she sniveled.

"I dreamed of this day since junior high school. I have always dreamed of marrying you, Zack." Nikki seemed to be settling down as she spoke. "Please come back and make love to me. Please come back and be my husband," she implored softly.

Once again, at nineteen years old one does not notice that she did not address the question about Pete. She did not deny it or admit any wrong doing. She also did not say that she loved me. She did not say that I was the only man in her life. She did not say that I was the only one she wanted to give herself to.

There are a million little things she could have said at that moment. "Please come back and be my husband," was probably the least intimate and the least endearing. But you don't think of that sort of stuff when you are just out of high school.

I made love to her gently at first that first time. But as the visions of Pete climbing through her bedroom window continued to whirl around in my head, I began to pound into Nikki violently. Bam, Bam, Bam, Bam... the head board smacked into the wall as I slammed into her every bit as savage as I had fucked Krysta that third time yesterday. As I recalled Krysta humping back and her deep guttural moans of pleasure, I smiled broadly as I emptied my balls into Nikki's belly.

As I laid there panting for air afterward, I was pleased that I had given my virginity to Krysta yesterday. At that moment, I didn't even care anymore if Pete had fucked Nikki first. "What are you smiling about," Nikki whispered in my ear while she kissed my neck. "I'm happy that I saved my virginity for the right person," I whispered back. "That's sweet," Nikki purred.

Nikki and I had a quick three day honeymoon before she had to travel across the state to her college. We had a wonderful time with simple excursions to the local amusement park, the county petting zoo and the state art museum. Although Nikki seemed less interested in sex, she was responsive when I made advances to her. I would have to say that she is far behind her mother when it comes to passion, intimacy and ability. But I was just happy to finally have her in my bed after all these years.

<<O>>

The first year couple of months were a bit rocky to put it politely. I made the trip from Woodinville across state to the University in Pullman to spend the Halloween weekend with Nikki. We had stayed in contact over the two months with phone calls and text messages. It was quite a surprise when I arrived at the campus and none of her new girlfriends even knew she was married. Nikki assured me it was no big deal. She insisted that she just wanted to fit in with all the girls her age and the majority of them were single.

The weekend was not nearly as intimate as I had hoped for. Nikki seemed more interested in hanging out with her new friends and claimed that she felt embarrassed about spending the nights in a motel.

"Now my friends are all gonna think I'm some sort of slut," she told me at one point. The words felt like a slap in the face. "So, you would be a slut for sleeping with your husband, but it was okay to pretend I don't exist?" I growled back. She gave me the first ever blow job from her that night. I guess it was her idea of making up.

For Thanksgiving, Nikki made the drive home for the holiday. But as soon as she was at the door on Wednesday night, she announced that she would be going back to Pullman on Saturday. She was very playful that night when we went to bed. She teased me about how hot her girlfriends thought I was. "I bet every one of them wish they were spreading their legs for you right now," she laughed wickedly as I mounted her. It seemed that their lustful desires had aroused Nikki. She was much more passionate than usual that evening.

That passion continued Thursday night after our families got together for Thanksgiving dinner. It was the first time that she had been the aggressor. Ripping my clothes off and climbing on top to ride me like a cowgirl. So it was quite a surprise for me when she suddenly announced

Friday morning that she was packing to go back. I had heard her cell phone ring when I was in the shower. She told me that one of her girlfriends needed a ride back to school because her car broke down.

After Thanksgiving, her phone calls home seemed to fall off drastically. She would call once each week and maybe text me quick little notes occasionally. I was so busy with working full time and taking night classes at the local University that the importance of this growing chasm escaped me completely. But I did notice it and it did make me feel uneasy.

Nikki again made the trip home for Christmas. But although her original plan had been to stay home till after the New Year, she only stayed home four days and then went back to Pullman on Sunday evening.

This time, my feelings were very hurt. This time, I told her that I felt like everyone else in her life was more important than me. Nikki insisted that it was just an emergency. She gave me another blow job before she left.

I tried to call Nikki on New Year's Eve to wish her well, but I was not able to get past her voice mail. She never answered my messages until the morning of the 3rd of January. She told me that her battery had gone dead and she had not realized it until she noticed that she had not received any calls in over four days.

I was now beginning to wonder if this long distance marriage would work out. I was still so busy with work and my own classes that it made it impossible to run across the state to spend more time with my new wife. I could feel the chasm growing with each passing week. It was a relationship that had already been marred by Pete's attempt to tear us apart. It was becoming very clear that the damage he had done had changed our relationship far beyond my first impression.

Chapter 4

I was deeply disappointed when I received a message from Nikki on the first week of February. She had called to tell me not to come over to Pullman for Valentine's Day because she was going to be too busy with school activities and we would not have very much time to spend together. It really bothered me that she called during a time when she knew that I would be in my evening classes with my cell phone off.

When I called her back the next evening between classes, her phone announced that user was unavailable which is what happens when the phone is turned off. I quickly called the pay phone in the hallway of her dormitory. It was a friendly voice that answered the phone, she told me she would go see if Nikki was available.

"Poor jerk, doesn't he know?" I heard a muffled voice in the background. "I don't get it, her husband is so much hotter than that other guy that comes up here," another voice stated. "Yeah, he even tried to put the move on me at the New Year's party," a third voice chimed in. "He thinks he's a big shot since he works at his daddy's car lot and drives a fancy red corvette," she added.

At that instant, I knew they were talking about Pete. I had seen him recently driving out of the mall parking lot with gorgeous blonde next to him in his new red corvette. It became instantly clear to me why Nikki has rushed off to go back to school on her last three visits home for the holidays. My stomach was in a knot as I hung up the phone before the girl returned to tell me that Nikki was not available.

It was just getting dark as I pulled into the parking lot outside of Nikki's dormitory. I knew it might be a while for anything to happen. I knew that Pete would have to make his grand entrance so he could flash his fancy car and show all the girls how cool he is. I parked in the back of the lot where I would be out of sight. I was close to the second driveway exit, which would make it easy to follow them without him noticing me.

I gritted my teeth when I saw his car pulling into the lot. Part of me was still hoping that I might be wrong about all of this. Moments later, I saw Nikki in his arms, kissing him and then she got into his corvette. I was glad that I quickly thought to take a photo of them kissing. Pete was very predictable after that. He did not waste time taking her out to dinner or a dance. They drove directly to the nearest fleabag motel. I took photos of him fondling her ass while he was renting the room. I took photos of them kissing each other when he stopped to get his overnight bag out of the car. I took photos of Nikki patting his ass while he opened the door to let them into room 18.

It was just after 7pm when I called Krysta. I was again filled with that vibrating rage that I felt that Saturday after the bachelor party. "Are you free to talk?" You could hear the quivering in my voice.

"Where are you, Zack?" I could hear the concern in her voice. Over the next several minutes, I told Krysta what I had seen. I told her about all the times Nikki ran off early during the holidays. "I'm pretty sure that she has never stopped seeing him," I told her hoarsely. "I'm so stupid," I moaned.

"YOU ARE NOT STUPID, ZACK!" It was the first time that Krysta had ever yelled at me. "You are a wonderful loving young man and you did your best to offer that love to her," she added softly. "Nikki is an idiot to have ruined that with her stupid infatuation with that shyster Pete," she snarled. "He's just like his old man," she added tersely.

Krystal then informed me that her husband had left that evening on a business trip to New York and would be gone for at least five days. "I could be there about midnight if I leave right now," I suggested hopefully. "I have a much better idea," Krysta announced cheerily. "We can meet at the cabin out by the lake. If we both leave now, we can be together in half the time," she offered. When I agreed to meet her at the cabin in Moses Lake, she told me where I could find the hidden key so I can go in and fire up the heating system and build a fire in the fireplace. "I'll bring everything else we will need," she added.

It took me just a little more than two hours to make the drive from Pullman to Moses Lake. There was very little traffic that evening and there weren't any speed traps along my route. The closer I got to the Lake, the more relaxed I became. I felt almost like a burden was falling away. I knew how safe I soon would feel with Krysta's arms around me. I knew exactly how wonderful it feels to *be* in her arms.

It was very chilly when I let myself into the house on the lake. I quickly went downstairs and ignited the pilot flame for the heating system and then set the controls once it was fired up. It would be a couple of hours before the system would heat the entire house to a comfortable temperature. So I went back upstairs to build a nice cozy fire in the large fireplace in the family room.

I was bent over the fire place stirring the logs with a poker when Krysta came into the house. "Oh God, look at you," she giggled playfully as she gawked at my butt bent over. "God, I've missed you," she gasped softly as she closed the door and began to remove her winter coat. "And look at you," I purred back as her chest came into view. The transparent white chiffon blouse made it clear that she had no bra on underneath. Her dark tan skin shined through the white fabric and her dark nipples were clearly visible to me.

Krysta dropped the duffle bag and her coat on the floor and walked directly to me. We fell together in a very passionate kiss as I lifted my hands to fondle her luscious breasts. "It has been so hard to not touch you," I gasped as we pulled apart. Thanksgiving, Christmas, and New Year were so difficult," I added as I kissed her again and then began to unbutton her blouse. "Yes, baby. I got so excited when we danced together," she moaned her reply. "I wanted you to do exactly what you are doing now." I could feel her body trembling as I bent forward to suck on her left nipple.

Krysta suddenly took a step back and I was amazed by how hard her nipples were. Because we were about eight feet from the fireplace, the chill in the air had made her nipples as hard as little rubber bullets. "I'll be right back," she announced as she turned and started for the hall leading to her bedroom. I marveled as I watched her walking down the hall topless. I was wondering how on Earth I could be so lucky to have such a sexy older woman who desired me so passionately.

Krysta was carrying an armful of blankets and pillows when she returned. "Mama Bird is gonna build a little love nest," she cooed in a seductive sort of tone. I just stood there and gawked at her half naked body as she spread the blankets out on the floor in front of the fireplace. "Don't just stand there! Get naked," she laughed when she noticed that I was staring at her.

I used my feet to wedge my shoes off while I was pulling my heavy winter sweater off over my head. I sort of lost my balance with the sweater around my head and had to hop on one foot to keep from falling down. I could hear Krystal laughing softly, even though the sweater was bunched around my head.

"Now THAT'S what I'm talking about!" she exclaimed playfully as I shoved my pants down and my dick bounced up against my belly.

"I should have fucked you after the wedding," Krysta whispered as her hand wrapped around my rigidness. "Maybe we could have saved you all this pain. "Ooooh God, I wanted to fuck you that night,"

I gasped as Krysta bent forward and swirled her tongue around the head of my dick. "You made my panties soaking wet when we danced that night," she moaned her reply as she gently pulled me down onto our little bed of blankets.

"I have to tell you… that I intend to have you as often as I can," Krysta murmured as she pushed me onto my back and straddled my cock. "Would you like that, lover?" she groaned as she impaled herself on my prick. "Oh, Gaaaawwwwd Yes," I gasped my reply. My heart skipped a beat because she had called me her lover. "Yesssss, I want to be your lover," I moaned as I reached up to fondle her luscious 34DD jugs.

Squish, Squish, Squish… in the silence of the cabin, I could hear the wetness in her pussy as she rocked back and forth on my prick. I lifted my head and reveled in the sensation of her firm silicone tits mashed against my face as she rode me like I was a stallion. "Gaaaawwwwd, I love fucking you," Krysta moaned throatily when I started nibbling on her nipples.

As Krysta bounced up and down with abandon, it crossed my mind that I have never experienced this lust or this hunger when Nikki and I mated. It has always seemed like Nikki was just performing her wifely chore. In all honesty, Nikki is woefully inadequate. I didn't realize that I was now grinning as I pulled Krysta down to kiss her.

"What's so funny?" she chuckled when I let her up. "I was just thinking how much hotter Mama bird is compared to baby bird," I told her while I playfully pulled on her left nipple. "I'm thinking she is a complete idiot," Krysta grunted as she pounded down harder. "And I'm the lucky one to have you," she moaned as she had a small climax course through her.

I rolled Krysta onto her back with my cock still buried inside. "Oooooh, Gawd yes," She growled as I lifted her feet back near her head and drove in as far as my 9 inch dick could reach. I felt her fingers digging into my ass while I pulled out a little and then rammed back in. It electrified me to see the hunger in her face as she pulled me even further inside and rolled her eyes back into her head. "Gaawd, I love your dick," she moaned.

As Krysta's body began to jerk and convulse beneath me, her pussy clamped down with each spasm creating a delicious jolt down the entire length of my prick. "Ooooooh, Fuck yes, Fuck yes," I groaned as my dick ejaculated several huge wads of semen deep into Krysta's vagina. "I'll never... get tired... of how delicious... that feels," Krysta panted as she gasped for air.

Krysta and I made love again before we finally fell asleep cuddled beside the fireplace. Again, it was much more intimate than anything I have ever felt with Nikki. "How can it be so wonderful with you and so lousy with... little bird?" I whispered just before we dozed off. "Because she's too dazzled with meaningless superficial affections to see how priceless a real relationship might be," Krysta answered very softly. She kissed me on the back of the neck and added. "But I do see how priceless you are."

Chapter 5

Krysta was in the kitchen when I woke up in the morning. Although the heat had finally warmed up the house to a comfortable level, she had left a terry cloth robe for me next to our little love nest by the fireplace. I was just tying the belt around my waist as I entered the kitchen. Krysta was talking to someone on her cell phone as I went to the counter to pour myself some coffee.

"Yes... he was wonderful! It was the best Valentine's Day gift ever," she told the listener. "Yes... that was a good one too... but this was special." Krysta glanced over at me and smiled broadly. "It's a night I will never forget." She puckered her lips and blew me a kiss after she said that. After some giggling and a whisper I couldn't make out, Krysta announced that it was time to go. "I'll call you tonight, Hun... I love you too." Then, she hung up.

I felt a wiggle between my legs when she stood up to come over to me. Her robe was completely open in front since she did not bother to tie the belt. "Bill says hello," she announced as she bent forward to kiss my cheek. "He... knows... I'm here?" I stammered as she stepped back. "Of course! I called him last night so he wouldn't worry when he called the house.

I could feel a huge knot twisting in my gut. My dick was no longer rigid. "What if he... figures out... we cheated?" I panted. I was breathing so deeply that I was suddenly dizzy. I quickly sat at the table fearing my knees would buckle any moment. "Don't be silly," Krysta laughed. "It's not cheating if he knows about it and approves." My mouth fell open and I stared blankly as that statement whirled through my brain. How on Earth could a 40 year old man be okay with his wife banging a kid more than half his age?

Krysta smiled slightly as she saw the confusion on my face. "It's really okay. Bill loves how horny I am after you and I have been together," she chuckled. "You make me so hot that I fuck his brains out every time I have been anywhere near you." It felt like the nightmare was growing somehow. In between the words of her last statement was the fact that he has been aware of this for some time now. "How long has he known?" I murmured. The words practically stuck in my throat.

"He has known everything since that Saturday before the wedding," she announced. "We don't have secrets and we share every detail," she added cheerily. "YOU'RE SHITTING ME! EVERY DETAIL?" I just blurted it out. Although I had never planned on having a secret affair, it HAD felt like a secret. It had felt like my safe haven. My only place on Earth that I could let my emotions out freely. "How could you?" I moaned hoarsely. "I told you things I've never told anyone."

I was struggling to pull away from her, but she clamped her arms around me tighter. "It's not like that," she told me softly. "I did not tell him what we talked about or said to each other. I would never share the feelings that you only shared with me." She assured me. "I only told him about the sex. I only told him how aroused, I got, whenever we were together and we couldn't do anything about it." Krysta bent forward and kissed my cheek. "It makes him crazy with lust and we fuck like wildcats every time," she giggled softly.

My body began to relax a bit, but my brain was still dizzy searching for answers that my life experience had no answers to. Although I am not a stupid young man, there are just so many things that I have not yet experienced in life. What Krysta had said about cheating, sort of made sense, and yet it was beyond my belief that any man could be okay with his wife banging another man. It was even more curious to me that he would enjoy her telling him about the sex.

The kaleidoscope of emotions that were racing across my face must have been very obvious to Krysta. She suddenly stood up and pulled me to my feet. "Come, let's talk, Hun," she suggested softly. My legs still felt oddly weak as she led me out to the couch in the living room. "Let's sit here so we can be comfortable," she whispered as she guided me down onto the couch. She left briefly to go bring out our coffee. She sat close to me, but not quite touching. She was angled so that she was facing me. Her robe was still wide open.

When Krysta had said we were going to talk, what she really meant was that she would do some talking and I would listen as best I could while my mind tried to keep up with all the new information. All of the new concepts and alternate life decisions that people can evidently pursue. Krysta talked for over an hour. She told me about her marriage with George. She confided that they married right out of high school because she was pregnant with Nikki.

Krysta made it clear that they were deeply in love when they married and were ecstatic about having a child. But neither of them knew how that new responsibility would interfere with their intimate time. A new child and the process of working up the corporate ladder took many hours out of every day and drained more energy than either of them dreamed possible. By the time Nikki was five years old, they were still deeply in love, but the passion and intense lust had been eroded and they became bored.

At the end of that year, they were approached by a young couple their own age at the company Xmas party and invited to sneak away for a more private gathering. They had been curious enough to accept the offer. Since they had left Nikki at grand mom's house, they would not have to hurry home and they were both excited as they followed the couple to their home.

Two other couples arrived soon after and within a short period of time there was dancing and drinking and clothes started falling off. Bill and Krysta had been a bit shocked at first, but as the other couples started touching them and rubbing on them, they had become wonderfully aroused. That was the beginning of their swinging lifestyle. Along the way, Bill discovered that he particularly enjoyed watching other men with his wife. It thrilled him to be able to see the lust and pleasure on her face.

He found that he was always ravenous to have her afterward.

As the years progressed, they found that Bill would get just as aroused if Krysta shared her fantasies or little chance sexual urges that might occur. Bill had been very aroused when she told him about our first hookup in my van. She confided that he was insatiable after the wedding when he saw me dancing with her while he remembered that I had savagely fucked her less than 24 hours before. She confessed that he got just as excited when we were all together for Thanksgiving and Christmas. She told me that he had considered having me over for New Year's Eve, but couldn't figure out how to make that look natural with all the rest of our family in attendance.

<<O>>

I was speechless when she finished talking. I had been staring at her gorgeous tits for most of the last ten minutes or so. I wasn't even aware that she was done until she cleared her throat to get me to look up. "So... what do you think of all this?" she asked softly. "I think you have the most beautiful tits I've ever seen," I joked to lessen my uneasiness. "No more tits till you tell me how you feel about this," she growled at me as she pulled her robe closed. But I noticed that she had a slight grin as she said it.

"I don't really know how I feel," I started tentatively. "That was a lot of information and a huge look into your marriage and your private matters," I explained. "It doesn't change how I feel about you in the least." That revelation sort of surprised me. "I'm still chewing on the not cheating aspect of this... I'm trying to figure out how that might apply to my situation." I confided. "I feel like I am cheating on Nikki, but I just don't give a shit because she's been banging Pete since before we got married."

"It thrills me that you desire me. That has been my only saving grace from the fucked up situation with Nikki." I had to stop for a moment as that truth hit me like a ton of bricks. "I have felt so lucky that I have you to turn to," I confessed. "If Bill is okay with that... then I truly am very lucky," I added softly. Krysta's

Robe again fell open as she scooted into my arms and practically sucked the life out of me. "You can have these tits anytime you like," she told me as she scooted forward and pressed them into my face.

Krysta rode my cock for nearly half an hour after that, then called Bill to tell him all about it. She was resting against my chest as she talked to him. I kissed her neck and fondled her breasts the entire time.

Afterward, she told me that she had been afraid that I might stop seeing her when I found out that she and Bill are singers. When I told her that I thought it was really hot, she nearly sucked the life out of me.

<<O>>

We decided to watch the local news while Krysta finally started breakfast. There had been more than a foot of snow overnight and we needed to see if there was any more snow that might be coming our way so we could stock up with food if necessary. While Krysta was cooking, I went out on the patio and brushed the snow out of the satellite dish. Then we took our food into the living room so we could watch the local news.

While we were waiting for the weather report, there were several local stories that were covered first. Several weather related auto accidents, a gang related shooting in a nearby town, and a grand opening of a new grocery store. I almost choked when Pete's face suddenly filled the TV screen. *"Son of Auto Giant to wed local Beauty Queen,"* was announced cheerily by the reporter. The beauty queen was none other than Katelyn Allison, who I have known since grade school.

"Looks like Nikki has some competition," Krysta laughed. "Yeah... but it didn't stop Pete from banging her last night," I rasped my answer. "I wonder if Kate has any clue where he was on Valentine's night," I muttered softly. My mind was racing with thoughts of how I could get even with him by telling Kate about all his dirty deeds. "Not my place to be the one," I thought out loud. "I would never hurt Kate like that," I added. Krysta brushed my cheek with her fingertips. "Yes, baby, it's better to let karma catch up with him. He'll get his someday," she whispered softly.

It ended up that we did get more snow that Sunday afternoon. Krysta and I just managed to get to the local grocery store and back to the lake just before the snow flurries started. We watched some TV shows until the satellite again filled with snow. Krysta then announced that she had some "family video, DVD's that we could watch.

Chapter 6

"Oooooh Geeeeezus," I gasped when the first video flashed onto the screen. The man on the screen was Mr. Johnson, my 9th grade math teacher. He was eating Krysta's pussy while Bill was fucking his wife Gloria up the ass. In the background, you could see two other couples engaged in various sex acts. None of them were coupled with their own spouse.

"Our parties tend to get a little... wild," Krysta giggled as she began to fondle my quickly swelling prick. "Gloria just loves a good hard cock up her ass," she laughed. "Have you... ever tried that?" she added with curiosity in her voice. My dick was now raging hard. "Gaaaawwwwd, I love to try," I groaned as some precum oozed out onto the back of Krysta's hand.

As Krysta led me to the bedroom holding my dick like it was a handle, she wagged her ass back and forth. "This is another first I get to do with you," she pointed out in a naughty sort of voice. "Front or back?" she inquired as she shrugged her robe off to the floor. "On your knees... at the foot of the bed," I growled. My dick was already pulsating from the excitement that I'm about to bang my first ass.

Krysta shot me a surprised playful look as she crawled onto the bed as requested. "I may not have done this before... but I've seen it on pornos." I told her as I reached down to spread her ass cheeks apart with both hands. "Oooooh, Zack," she moaned as I licked my tongue all the way up her crack and then used my tongue to tickle her little rosebud. "Yesssssss, Zack... Yessssss," she groaned when I began to burrow my tongue up into her rectum. "Ooooh, gawd that's good," Krysta bellowed.

I continued to tongue fuck her ass for a couple of minutes while I slowly added a finger to probe inside and then a second finger. Once I had her loosened up, I drag my dick up and down her drenched pussy a couple of times to get it good and lubricated. With the precum that was oozing from my peephole, my cock slipped into her anus nice and smooth.

"Ooooooh, Zaaaaaaaack," Krysta moaned as I slowly shoved my cock all the way up her ass. It was a very deep, husky gasp that sounded like she was possessed. "Ooooh, fuck that's good," I groaned my reply. The sensation of her hot tight ass squeezing my prick was exquisite. "I'm gonna want a lot of this," I groaned as my legs vibrated from the excitement.

I very slowly pulled all the way out till just the knob was left inside and then very slowly drove back in. I wanted to remember every electrifying moment of this first time. I could feel Krysta's ass cheeks quivering as I once again impaled her ass. "It's s-o-o-o-o-o big," she groaned. I fucked her very slowly like this for several minutes until her rectal muscles finally relaxed and her cheeks stopped quivering.

"Fuck me, harder... harder," Krystal bellowed in that deep throaty voice. "Bam, Bam, Bam... I pounded into her so forcefully that the headboard slammed against the wall. "Give it to me, Give it to me, Give it to me," Krysta grunted with each savage thrust. I held her waist firmly as I rutted into her over and over.

My legs vibrated uncontrollably as I emptied my seed into her hot clenching rectum. "Oh my god, that's good! S-o-o-o-o-o good...s-o-o-o-o-o good," I bellowed. It thrilled me to see my thick white jism oozing from her ass pucker when I slid my dick out of her. "I bet you'll remember this forever," she giggled playfully. "Ooooooh yes! Yesssss," I groaned my reply.

I cleared the satellite dish out again after dinner and threw some more logs on the fire. Although the house was plenty warm with the heater on, we both enjoyed the flickering ambience of the fireplace. We have already decided to sleep there again tonight cuddled on our little bed of blankets. It just seemed so wonderful to cuddle with Krysta there.

We got a little more information concerning the engagement of Pete and Katelyn on the evening news. The journalist reported that they had been high school sweethearts which was a crock of shit since Kate had dated Brad Biggs the entire three years of high school. She had believed that the star quarterback would make a good husband and afford her the sort of life she desired. The only reason that Kate ended up available was that Brad dumped her when he got his full scholarship to a major university in Texas.

It was also reported that Pete had proposed on Valentine's Day just before leaving town for a business venture. "Yeah... he had some business to take care of," I growled at the TV. "Had a secret out of town deposit to make," I added as I glanced over at Krysta. In the back of my mind, I was appalled that Pete could propose to Kate in the morning and then go fuck my wife in the evening. "I hope karma kicks his ass," I groaned.

Krysta was sucking my cock when her cell phone started buzzing next to us on the floor. When I glanced down, I saw Bill's face as the caller ID photo. "It's Bill," I groaned softly as her head continued to bob up and down. "Answer it," she blurted quickly, then shoved my dick into her mouth again. "Hello, this is Zack," I announced meekly.

"Is your dick in my wife's mouth?" Bill laughed heartily. "Yes... ugh... it is," I replied. I was amazed that Bill could be so cavalier about his wife sucking another guy's dick. "HA-HA-HA-HA... Your wife can't come to the phone because my dick's in her mouth," Bill was laughing hysterically. "Just like Danny DeVito in that movie... ha-ha-ha-ha." I am way too young to have any idea what Bill was referring to, but Bill was laughing so hard that it was obvious that he thought it was hysterically funny.

I shivered a little as I felt some of Krysta's drool running down the length of my prick. It amazed me that my cock seemed even harder than before the call. "Doesn't my sweetie give good head?" Bill boasted with a chuckle. "Ooooh, Gawd yes," I moaned as she licked all the way up the shaft and then engulfed the crown with her lips. "Okay then, tell her to give me a call... when she's not... engaged," he laughed. As I hung up the phone, I was again astounded that Bill could be so okay with all of this.

"Are you ready for some pussy, baby?" Krysta giggled as she stood up and straddled my saliva drenched boner. "Ooooh, Fuck Yes," I groaned as she impaled herself on my prick. Krysta's pussy was so saucy that her fluids were running down my thighs and I could hear squishy noises as she rocked back and forth. I reached forward and twisted gently on both her nipples. I was so aroused by knowing that Bill knew I was drilling his wife that I flooded her pussy with my semen very quickly.

We were both panting for air side by side on the couch when the phone rang again. This time it was my phone on the coffee table.

"It's your daughter," I announced when I glanced down and saw Nikki's photo on the caller ID. "By all means... answer it," Krysta laughed as she rolled closer to cuddle up. "I'm so sorry that I missed you yesterday," Nikki greeted me. "I just... got busy," she said softly. "And who did you get busy with?" I growled playfully. "Just... a friend," she groaned her lie.

"Oh, believe me... I know how busy you've been." I growled back. Now, my anger was getting the better of me. "I know WHO you've been busy with as well," I yelled. "I know what you did on your birthday night and on prom night. I know who visited you for Thanksgiving and New Year's. AND, I know exactly where you were last night." I was practically screaming now. "How? Could you possibly... think?"

Before she could finish, I cut her off. "I'M NOT THINKING!" I yelled. "I was at your dorm last night and I saw you kissing on Pete when you got into his car. I saw Pete fondling you while you checked in at that flea bag motel. I saw you grabbing his ass while he let you into your motel room." There was only silence from the other end of the phone now.

"Your mother saw Pete sneaking out of your bedroom window at 2am on your birthday night," I told her candidly. "You remember that... the night you lost your virginity," I shouted. "She also saw him leaving at 3am on prom night. The same night that you wouldn't go to a hotel with me because you said that you wanted to save yourself for our wedding night." There was still silence from her end as I completed my tirade. "And, I know who visited you for Thanksgiving and New Year's because your dorm mates talk too loud when the phone is dangling on the wall."

I could hear Nikki beginning to sob on the other end of the phone. "DON'T YOU DARE CRY," I screamed.

"You have no right to cry," I growled. "You gave up that right when you gave your virginity to Pete." I was so angry that my body was quivering. "You gave up that right when you married me and continued all this shit afterward," I screamed. "Don't you fucking act like you care now!" I hung up before Nikki could say anything else.

Krysta just held me in her arms for quite some time after I hung up the phone. It felt a bit surreal to be in the arms of my wife's mother completely naked. Part of me felt like I was doing the same thing that Nikki was doing. "I feel like I am cheating too," I whispered miserably. Krysta gently kissed the side of my neck. "It's not cheating since she obviously has never intended to be faithful," Krysta told me softly. "She should never have married anyone if she intended to be Pete's fuck buddy," she added.

"Will you... still want to see me... if I divorce her?" I whispered. Krysta gently lifted my head to gaze directly into my eyes. "I will always want to see you, baby," she told me plainly. "Bill and I will welcome you in our home any time you like," she added as she bent forward to kiss my cheek. "I still don't quite understand that," I confided. "That Bill is okay with that."

Krysta spent the next several minutes telling me that she and Bill loves each other very deeply and they have chosen to live a very different lifestyle than most couples. "We found out early on that we both loved having sex with other people around watching," she confided. "As time progressed, we found that it was incredibly erotic to allow others to join us in sex and that led us into joining a group of swingers." she confided.

"But that's different than you... meeting me for sex," I whispered. Krysta smiled broadly as she bent forward to kiss me again. "That's because Bill loves how I fuck his brains out every time I have been anywhere near you," she laughed cheerily. "He loves how happy you make me and he loves how I share that with him when I get home." After Krysta kissed me again and pulled me closer into her arms, she told me that Bill would love it if I would spend some nights at their house when he is home. "He would be perfectly happy to sleep in the guest bedroom if you'd like to spend the night." She added. After that, we cuddled on our bed of blankets and made love. It was an intimate and tender mating. We slept in each other's arms and I felt much better.

Chapter 7

I met Katelyn Allison on the first day of first grade. She was a tiny little red head girl with the whitest skin I had ever seen. She picked me out instantly to be her protector since I was the biggest boy in the class.

She picked out the chair right next to mine and informed me that she would be my best friend if I would be hers. At the end of the day, I found that she lived only two blocks from my parent's house. I found out that her mother Abigale drove a Chrysler minivan and that Abigale tends to always be late no matter what the appointment might be.

I waited with Katelyn that first day of school until her mother came to pick her up twenty minutes late.

Abigale was a fiery redhead with more energy than I had ever seen in single mother and she seemed to accept me as Katelyn's buddy from the moment she met me. When I informed her that I was walking home, she insisted on driving me home. For the next six years, I rode home in the back of that little minivan every day. Kate and I became very close friends.

In junior high school, things changed a little for Kate and me. She sort of fell into a clique of girls and I got interested in sports. We still considered ourselves close friends, but we had a few classes together and much of our free time was taken up by our new activities. We would sometimes dance with each other at school dances and often ate lunch together. But we really did not have any alone time during those years. I think as a result of that, I never really did have any sort of romantic intentions about her. I did, however, notice what a stone fox her mother was.

Things changed drastically between me and Kate during the first week of high school. Over the summer, Kate had met a boy named Brad Biggs, who had just moved here from Texas. They had begun dating and she was quite smitten with this rich athletic young man. On the first day of school, Kate had run into me in the hallway and kissed me on the cheek because she was happy to see a familiar face in our new school.

When Brad suddenly came around the corner and saw her kissing me, he was not happy. He ran up and got in my face and told me that if he ever saw me near his girlfriend again, he would beat me senseless.

Although he was quite a bit more muscular than me, I was at least four inches taller and I was in my second year of wrestling. I had calmly stepped back and told him to take his best shot. "Let's just get this out of the way right now," I taunted him. When he took a swing at me, I easily dodged it and swept his legs out from under him using his own momentum to body slam him onto the marble floor.

The impact of the floor, knocked the wind out of him and left him stunned. "This isn't over," he groaned as I walked away. But two things happened that day that changed everything for me and Kate.

The first was that Kate felt sorry for Brad and thus agreed to his demand that she not talk to me anymore. The second was that Brad had one of the senior football players track me down in the locker room and beat the daylights out of me. Although the beating was humiliating, the deepest hurt was that Kate never once said she was sorry it happened.

The closest I got to an apology happened three years later. It was the week before Nikki and I got married. Kate called me to wish me well with the wedding. During the call, she informed me that things were over with Brad and she would like it if we could be friends again. "I really am sorry for what happened and I'd really like my friend back," she told me. I politely thanked her for the call and told her any friendship would have to start all over.

It did not surprise me in the least when I saw Pete's mom and dad in many of the sex DVD's that Krysta shared with me over the next several weeks. I did in fact take Bill's offer to come and spend the night on several occasions. There were two nights that she Krysta spent the night at my apartment and we made a video of our sex play to email to him. Once I got over the initial shock of Bill being in the same room while I fucked his wife, I found that it really aroused me to have someone watching.

Krysta brought some of their swinging videos over to my house. When I was sorting through the pile after she went home, I found two

DVD's that were different from all the rest. Different color sleeves and different hand writing. For some reason, Pete's father's name was on the outside of those two sleeves.

I was shocked when I watched them both alone in my apartment.

The first video started out as a little get together that Tom (Pete's dad) had arranged under the pretense that he was planning a surprise birthday party for his wife June. The only two people with Tom in that kitchen was Krysta and Kate's mom Abigale. Within fifteen minutes, it became obvious that the women had been drugged by the drinks they were given.

Suddenly there were half a dozen men in the kitchen. None of those men had ever appeared in any of the other swinger party videos I had watched. By the way the women were acting, I would guess that they were given something that made them very horny and lowered their inhibitions. They were taken to Tom's bedroom and stripped naked. Then the men took turns fucking both of the women. Except for Tom. He was only interested in banging Kate's Mom. He fucked her three times over the next hour.

The second video was recorded inside a motel room. When the door opened and Tom led Abby into the motel room, I was pretty surprised that it was her. But it became very clear that Tom had blackmailed her to this room with threats to show the party video he had made with all those other men. Abby had a look of disgust on her face the entire time that Tom rutted into her. She calmly got dressed and left immediately after he was through. She never said a single word.

When I called Krysta to tell her what I had seen, she told me that she had placed those there so I would know what a devious prick Pete's dad was. She also confessed that she and Bill had tricked Tom into giving them the videos by giving them video of Krysta banging me. They had told him that she tricked me into fucking her and had no idea the video was being recorded.

"I hope you will forgive us," she whispered. I told Krysta that if it had helped to get Abby out of Tom's blackmailing hold that I was proud to be involved. "I'll make sure she knows that," Krysta told me with a chuckle. "She may want to thank you personally," she added in a naughty sort of tone. Then, she revealed that Abby's husband Bob had been in on the initial "party arrangement" so he could bang one of the other men's wives on the same evening at a hotel downtown.

Krysta also informed me that this had all happened more than a year ago and that Pete's parents are no-longer invited to their swinger events. ALL of the couples in the group agreed to outcast them due to Tom's blackmailing behavior. Abby had divorced Bob six months ago when she learned of his involvement which made her have to hook up with Tom on a half dozen more occasions. When Tom tried to blackmail Krysta, she had handed the phone to Bill and he told Tom to fuck himself. They also told him they would put his party video on the internet so everyone could see that he had drugged the women.

<<O>>

At 5 feet 4, Abigale is two inches taller than Kate. Her 34DD-22-32 body is surprisingly voluptuous for such a small woman. At 39 years old her skin is still milky white and smooth as cream. Her flaming red hair reaches nearly to her waist and she seems even sexier to me than when I was a young teenager.

I never in a million years would have ever dreamed that I would someday have sex with her.

I met Abby at a fancy suite hotel in the downtown area on Saturday afternoon. She had called me and told me she wanted to see me and thank me for helping her. "Bring some swimming trunks," she told me, "And something nice to wear for dinner." I was amazed by the opulence of the hotel suite. It had a living room, a kitchen, a huge master bedroom with oversized king size bed and a gigantic bathroom that included a Jacuzzi large enough to fit four people.

I could hear the water running in the bathroom when Abby let me into the room. She was wearing just a white chiffon robe that was very short and transparent. "I told you to bring the trunks in case you felt modest," she giggled as she raised up on her tip toes to kiss my cheek. Her robe fell open as she stepped back. "But I will be bathing nude," she added with a playful grin. My dick instantly swelled to erection as I gawked at her gorgeous naked body.

"Let's get in the tub, we have lots to talk about," she announced as she turned towards the bathroom.

"Don't be shy," she laughed. "I expect your dick to be hard so don't worry about THAT," she added. I was very happy that she had added it. I HAD been worried about exactly that! I quickly stripped my clothes off and threw them on the floor next to the small duffle bag of clothes I had brought for dinner.

"Look at you, Zack," she purred when she saw my 9 inch dick pulsating against my belly. "You certainly have grown up since the last time I saw you." She whispered as I stepped into the Jacuzzi. "Krysta tells me that you have some things to share with me about Pete." I felt her hand sliding into my lap. "But that can wait till after," she cooed as her hand began to fondle my dick. "Oooooh gawd yes," I groaned my agreement.

Abby stood up and straddled my lap. "Krysta says that big dick feels wonderful," Abby growled as she began to lower herself onto my throbbing prong. "Ooooh, Gawd, that's good," she groaned as her cunt engulfed my prick. I could feel her body trembling when she finally came to rest with her ass cheeks pressed against my thighs. "Gaaaaaw-wwwwd, you're huge," she moaned.

I bent my head forward and started sucking hungrily on both of her perfectly round hooters. "I always wanted to do this," I moaned while I slobbered all over both her tits. "I know, baby… I saw how you looked at me," she laughed. "It always made my panties wet," she confided. I was mesmerized by Abby's gorgeous body as she bounced up and down with abandon. I was ecstatic that Kate's mom had also desired me… that she was giving herself to me.

I had both hands grasping her ass cheeks when I felt her vibrating near climax. Abby had been humping me for over twenty minutes, but seemed like she was having trouble making it over the edge. I slid my right hand down the crack of her butt and slowly slipped a finger into her tight ass pucker. "OH YES, OH

ZAAAAAAAAACK… YESSSSSSSSSS," she screamed. Her body went completely rigid and then began to jerk as she got off. "Oh, Fuck Fes… Fuck Yes," I groaned my reply as my cock flooded her vagina with my thick white jizz.

It was a fancy upscale Italian restaurant that Abigale took us to in her Silver Mercedes coupe. Heads turned as we were escorted to our private table in the back. Part of that was due to our difference in age and height. At six foot three, I am nearly a foot taller than Abby. But the other reason they were staring was that Abby looked breathtaking in the very tight black jersey dress she was wearing. The way her tits were pressed tightly against the soft tight jersey fabric, it was obvious that she was not wearing a bra. I had my suspicions that she probably had no panties either.

I got an immediate affirmation to my suspicion as she sat down while I held her chair. Abby lets her legs spread apart just enough as she sat down that I saw her smooth bare gash for just a brief moment. "OH, Fuck Me," I gasped softly. "Yes, honey... you will," she giggled. "But first we're gunna have dinner," she added with a playful wink.

After we ordered our meal and the waitress brought our drinks, Abby leaned forward slightly and smiled sweetly. "So... what was it you need to tell me about Pete?" she whispered as if it was a secret. My eyes were glued to her huge round jugs that were now resting on the table. Her nipples were erect and looked like pencil erasers pressed against the soft fabric. "First... can I say that you are the sexiest woman I have ever seen?" I groaned my reply. Abby just smiled and winked.

Over the next ten minutes or so, I told Abby all about Pete. I told her about how he took Nikki's virginity and then had her again on prom night. I told her about the bachelor party and how he tried to make it look like I was having sex with the strippers. And I told her about how he has continued to see Nikki up at the college in Pullman. "So that's how you started seeing Krysta?" she asked softly. "Yes... and she has been wonderful," I answered without hesitation or embarrassment.

While we were eating desert, Abigale asked me what had happened between me and Katelyn. "I always sort of thought that you two would end up together," she added. I told Abby about the first week in high school. How Brad had forbade her to be friends with me anymore and how he had one of his football buddies beat me up. "The only thing that really hurt was that she never once said she was sorry about all of that," I told her softly at the end. "It sort of... broke my heart," I whispered. That was the very first time that I had finally admitted that to myself.

Abby was sucking my cock in the living room when Krysta and Bill arrived at our hotel suite. Abby had invited them to join us because she also wanted to thank them for helping her break the blackmail with

Pete's dad. It sort of thrills me as they walked in and Abby continued to suck me off as if it was a daily occurrence. "Get naked and join us," she announced as she raised her head for a moment and then resumed sucking me.

I could see that Bill's eyes were glued to Abby bent over sucking me off with her lily white ass hanging out the back of her short jersey dress. Krysta was staring at me with a goofy smile on her face. "Save some of that for me," she told Abby while she was stripping her clothes off.

As soon as they were naked, Abby stood up and led Bill to the bedroom using his prick like it was a handle. "He's all yours," Abby called back to Krysta. "I've heard you have been dreaming about this for quite some time," I heard her whisper to Bill. "Oooh, Gaaaawwwd Yes," Bill groaned when she pressed him onto the bed and mounted him like a cowgirl. I could hear the bed crashing against the wall as Krysta straddled my lap and sat down. "I hope she doesn't steal you away from me," Krysta moaned as she impaled herself on my prick. "Not even possible," I groaned back.

Chapter 8

It was the second week in March that Nikki finally called and tried to make up with me. She told me it had all been a huge terrible mistake. I reminded her that the mistake had happened on her 18th birthday when she gave her virginity to Pete instead of me. "It's over, I've already filed for the divorce," I told her. Then, I hung up.

Over the last two weeks, I had been spending the weekends with Bill and Krysta. But during the week, I was staying at my apartment since I was so busy with work all day and with classes in the evenings at the university. Although I only went to the college on Monday, Wednesday and Thursday, the other two nights I spent doing my homework and also completing some work tasks for my father.

Abby had become a regular visitor to my apartment on these two nights each week. She would show up, cook dinner for me and then read or watch TV quietly until I was ready for bed. Then, she would fuck my brains out. It was a Friday evening when I received a call from Katelyn. Abby and I had just crawled into bed. She was sucking my cock when I answered the call.

"Mom told me I should talk to you before I marry Pete," Kate announced. The annoyance in her voice was very plain. "Don't ask for something you don't want to know," I warned her. Before she could protest, I reminded her that no-one wanted to believe me when I said he lied about the bachelor party.

"What will make you believe me now?" I asked. "You didn't believe me then and you were supposedly my friend back then," I reminded her.

My legs were vibrating on the bed as Abigale continued to very slowly toy with my cock and suck on the knob. "Things... have changed," Kate whispered softly. "I'm beginning to see things in Pete... I don't like," she confessed hoarsely. "Okay! I'll tell you the truth," I growled. "And when you don't like it, you can just pretend it isn't true," I groused. "Just like when Brad had that guy beat me to a pulp." I added.

Over the next several minutes, I told her everything Pete had done since that first time he fucked Nikki on her birthday. When I told her exactly what really happened at my bachelor party, I reminded her that I had tried to tell her about it when she called before my wedding. So when I got to the part about what Pete did on Valentine's night, I sent her a visual aid so she could see the truth this time. "You can pretend those photos don't mean anything, but I was there," I told her after I sent the photos to her phone. "THAT... is the real Pete! That is the REAL guy you will be marrying."

I could hear that Kate was sobbing quietly when I finished. She quietly told me that she was sorry for everything that has happened. She told me that she knew I would not lie to her. Then she said she had to go. My body jerked and vibrated as I emptied my cock inside Abby's mouth. I sort of got a perverse thrill out of her sucking me the entire time I talked to her daughter. I rolled Abby on her back afterward and ate her pussy till she climaxed so hard that she wet herself. Then we went to sleep.

In the morning, I asked Abigale if I had been too harsh with Katelyn on the phone. She kissed me gently and told me that she had been amazed by how rational I had been given the pain that Pete has brought into my life. "Besides, she really needed to hear the non-sugar coated version," she added with a giggle.

I rolled Abby onto her back and rutted into her brutally while we kissed and mauled at each other. After I flooded her with my semen, I told Abby that I should thank him and his father for bringing us together.

Abby followed me out as I left for work. She said she'd be back next Tuesday.

There was a car parked in my parking space when I got home to my apartment after work. Although the vehicle seemed familiar to me, I could not quite remember where I knew it from. "Mom said you'd be home about now." The sudden voice startled me as I entered my apartment. The voice had come from Katelyn who was seated on my couch. "Mom told me where you hid the key for her," she added while I stood there with my mouth gaping open.

"What else... did she tell you?" I asked as I reached back to close the door behind me. "That I was insane to ever give up your friendship," she answered me without hesitation. It was difficult not to stare at

Kate, as I made my way towards her. I had not seen her since the prom night when she was the prom queen.

Her beautiful prom gown had covered most of her petite nubile body. I forgot how absolutely sexy she could be.

Katelyn was dressed in very tight low rider jeans. The sort that sits very low on the hips and allows you to see the waistband of her panties. Except, I could see no waistband present. The very tight sweater she was wearing just covered down to her belly button and the way her perky 32B tits were pressed against the fabric. It was obvious that she was not wearing any bra. It was taking all of my willpower to keep my dick from swelling up.

"To what do I owe this pleasure?" I asked sheepishly as I sat down next to Kate on the couch. In all those years that I had been friends with Kate, I had never thought of her in a sexual way. But now my mind was racing with images of what it would be like to strip her naked and sample that lovely nubile body.

"What would Pete think of you being here with me like this?" I added while I forced myself to sit a full arm's length away.

"I don't give a shit what Pete thinks anymore," Kate blurted out. "I am calling off the wedding as soon... as he gets back." Her voice trailed off as she became embarrassed about him being out of town again. The fact that his "business" was again in Pullman was fairly obvious to both of us. "I take it that you believe me now," I whispered.

In my heart, I felt empathy with Kate. I knew exactly how demoralizing and humiliating that knowledge felt inside of her. I have wrestled with those emotions many times over the last nine months. I had turned much of that into a rage. I had been fortunate enough to have Krysta in my life to hold me and help me through the pain.

"Let me start over," I whispered as I saw some tears welling up in Kate's eyes. "I am so sorry that I had to be the one to bring this to you," I told her as I reached over to place a hand on her leg. "I'm sorry that I was so harsh with you," I added. Kate suddenly slumped against me and began to sob. It was a deep bellowing flood of anguish as she released her pain. I simply held her in my arms and let her cry herself out just like Krysta had done for me on so many nights in the past.

"I need my friend back," she sniveled when she finally relaxed enough to speak. Her arms were wrapped around my neck and her head was on my chest. "I never stopped being your friend, Kate. I just had to live with not having you around anymore." Without really thinking about it, I bent my head down and kissed her on the top of the head. As I glanced down I could see her perky cone shaped tits pressed against the sweater and I felt a little wiggle between my legs.

"Ooooh, Zack... I need you in my life again," she sobbed again. But this time, she craned her neck and pressed her lips forcefully against mine and kissed me very passionately. "I was so stupid," she gasped softly. "I had the most wonderful guy in my life and I wasted that on guys like Brad and Pete." She kissed me again and I felt her hands move to hold my face. "I want you back in my life, Zack... I want you back in my life," she panted. For a brief moment, my hands had moved up and fondled her breasts. I quickly moved them away and leaned back away from her a bit.

I could see her eyes were focused between my legs and the bulge that was now pressing against my blue jeans. "I'm sorry...if I got...fresh," I whispered. Kate lifted her head and had the beginnings of a smile. I could see that both her pointy nipples were hard as little pebbles. "That was okay, Zack...it was...nice," she whispered back. My dick was throbbing now as I gazed into her emerald green eyes.

I scooted back a few more inches and placed my hand on top of hers because she had placed her hand on my knee. "Maybe we should discuss some...other details...before we go any further with this," I suggested softly. There was still a goofy expression on her face as she scooted a bit closer and a very noticeable sparkle in her now clear eyes.

"Mom told me about how you helped her out," she said it sort of coyly. "She told me...how close you've become." Her hand was now moving up my thigh towards the bulge in my jeans. "She also told me that you have the nicest cock she has ever sucked." My body jerked slightly as she rubbed her hand up and down the entire length of my throbbing boner.

As I lifted my hand, I slipped it up under her sweater and cupped her bare left breast. "Gawd, I've wanted to do this since seventh grade," I moaned into her mouth as I began to kiss her hungrily. The sensation of her perky cone shaped breast in the palm of my hand was electrifying. I really had dreamed of this day as far back as 7th grade. I just had never though it would ever be possible. I never considered that Kate would be interested in anything beyond our friendship.

It thrilled me even further when she unfastened my pants and began to jerk my dick while she continued to kiss me. I lifted her sweater off over her head and had to stop momentarily to gawk at her gorgeous cone shaped tits with the puffy pink areolas. "You are so fucking pretty, Kate," I gasped softly. "I want you to fuck me Zack," she whispered her reply.

I reveled in every second of watching her wiggle out of her sexy tight jeans. I actually giggled softly as I saw that I had been right about her not wearing any panties. "What's so funny," she asked as she pulled the jeans off her feet. "I sort of thought to myself that you weren't wearing any panties earlier," I chuckled while I kicked my jeans off too.

I paused for a moment to look at her young naked body. "I never dreamed that I would ever be naked with you," I groaned softly as I pulled her down onto the couch. Her soft, creamy skin felt like velvet, as her body pressed against mine. I kissed her greedily as I rolled her onto her back. My hands were gently mauling both of her nubile little tits. "My god, you are sexy," I groaned as I lifted up to again look at her naked body.

"Are you sure this is what you want?" I whispered as I crawled up to place my cock against the lips of her pussy. "More than anything on Earth," she replied as her hands grabbed my waist to pull me down. "Yes,

Fuck me, Zack... Fuck me," she moaned in a deep guttural voice as my dick slipped inside of her. We were both quivering with arousal as we kissed savagely and groped at each other's body.

The sensation of Kate's tight pussy gripping my prick as she impaled herself on it was exquisite. Nether of her two lovers had a cock larger than six inches and neither had been more than half as big around. I could feel Kate's pussy quivering as it stretched out to accommodate the three inches of girth that was invading her hot slippery hole. "Oh, Zaaaacccck," she moaned as my dick came to rest jammed against her cervix.

The sex with Krysta and with Abigale has been hot and steamy. Almost animalistic and primal. But with Kate it was entirely different. Maybe that's because we had been friends for so long and had developed much deeper feelings. Maybe it was because we had both harbored secret desires that we had never let bubble to the surface. The feelings that were exploding inside of me at this moment were overwhelming and yet addictively sweet.

I lifted up with my arms so I could watch my dick seesaw in and out of Kate's deliciously tight pussy. "Gawd, you're beautiful," I moaned as I gazed down at her young nubile body. It thrilled me to watch my dick disappearing into her drenched slit and how her cunt lips pulled gripped my dick and pulled upward each time I pulled back up. "Cum in me, Zack... fill my pussy up," she moaned.

As Kate began to writhe beneath me with her orgasm, I pressed my dick all the way into her quivering vagina and I kissed her passionately as my semen flooded deep into her womb. My cock spasmed three times and I could feel the sticky fluid oozing out of her pussy lips even with my dick jammed inside. I could see tears in her eyes as I lifted my head to look at her.

"No-one has ever made love to me like that," Kate whispered while she raised her hands to hold my face. "I am gonna want a lot more of that... if you'd be interested," she told me softly. "I've never felt like this before either," I confided and then kissed her on the forehead. "I definitely want as much of you as you are willing to give."

Krysta was disappointed when I called to inform her that I would not be coming over for the night as usual. But she was pleased for me that I had connected with Katelyn. She confided that she had always thought that Kate was a much better match for me than Nikki. "But please don't forget Bill and me," she pouted. "You have been so wonderful with us," she added.

Katelyn called Abigale and told her how we had connected to. Abby was thrilled by the news and told Kate that she was ecstatic that we had finally found our way into each other's arms. She told Katelyn that she had always believed that we belong together. Abby also told Kate that she would stop seeing me if we thought that might be an interference. Kate told her that we have already discussed that and that we had a plan that would include her.

Although Kate spent every night at my apartment for those last two weeks in March, she was busy during the weekdays with her new job as a lingerie model. I stayed busy with work and school studies.

On Tuesday's, I would visit Bill and Krysta in the evening for a couple of hours and on Thursday's I would visit Abigale at her home. It thrilled me each time that Kate would meet me at the door in one of her new negligees and make love to me as soon as I came back home.

On the first Saturday in April, Katelyn and I moved into the new Condo we had purchased together.

I took all of Nikki's belongings and stored them in the garage at Bill and Krysta's house. The divorce papers had already been served on Nikki several weeks before. Our new life together was beginning very nicely. We just had one more bit of the past to rectify.

Chapter 9

It was the second weekend in April that that Katelyn and I finally got even with our cheating partners. On Friday evening Kate and I checked into the Trailhead Motel out on the edge of town by the truck stop. Kate had disguised her voice to sound like Nikki to fool Pete into coming to the motel. He would be expecting Nikki to be waiting for him in room eighteen. She had told him to be there at 8pm and the door would be unlocked.

My dick was raging hard as Kate and I crawled onto the bed at ten minutes till eight in room eighteen. We were both naked and we kissed very passionately as we anticipated Pete's arrival at any moment.

Kate was perched on my rigid prick like facing the door when Pete came bursting into the room. That way Pete would have no trouble seeing that it was Kate riding my prick.

"I believe you remember, Zack," Kate goaded him as he stood there frozen in his tracks with his mouth gaping open. "You know... Nikki's husband.... she's the one you've been banging in Pullman." Kate never stopped riding my dick the entire time she was talking. I reached up and twisted on Kate's nipples as I felt her shivering into orgasm. As her body jerked on top of me, I flooded her with three huge wads of jism.

"You can go now... the show's over," Kate taunted Pete as she stood up from my lap. It thrilled me to see my semen running down her legs as Pete stood there gawking at her with his mouth still gaping wide open. "I can have any whore I want," Pete gasped pathetically. "That's right Pete... you can have Nikki and all the other whores you want," I yelled back. "But this lady is mine because you don't deserve her."

Pete opened his mouth like he wanted to say something, but nothing came out. "Maybe your dad will share some of his when your mom dumps him." I laughed at him. Pete had no idea that three women had visited his mother that afternoon. They had told her about how Tom had drugged them for sex and then blackmailed them just like he had with Abigale. They each provided DVD's that he had sent them to blackmail them with. When they left, Pete's mom was hysterical with anger.

It was just before 10pm when Nikki arrived home at Krysta's house. She was in a hurry because she had received a desperate text from Pete while she was driving. He hadn't said much except that they needed to talk. That something had changed. When she came bursting through the front door, she froze as if she had hit a brick wall.

"Come sit down before you fall down," Krysta told her softly. Nikki was glancing back and forth between Kate on my left and her mother on my right with me sitting between them on the couch. "Today is the day you get answers for your behavior," Katelyn informed her. Nikki was white as a ghost as she sat down in the love seat across from us.

Over the next several minutes, we all confronted her about how she had slept with Pete on several occasions before she married me. We all told her how selfish that was. To marry me even though she wanted Pete. Even though she intended to continue seeing Pete. Then, we showed her photos of Pete that we took over the last four weeks. Each of us had taken turns following him and had taken many photos of him taking other girls to hotel rooms. Many of the photos showed him groping the girls openly, even before they got there. "This is the man you have ruined your marriage for," Kate told her. "You can probably move in with him since you are not welcome here," Krysta told her daughter.

Nikki was horrified when she arrived at Pete's house. There were policemen there and for some reason Tom was in handcuffs. Peggy was tossing Tom's belongings out into the front yard and Pete was being restrained by one of the officers. "And be sure to charge this son-of-a-bitch for blackmail and sexual assault," Peggy screamed from the front door. In her hand were a half dozen DVD's. I have all the proof you'll need right here. "And you can take my son too. You will see that he is an accomplice in many of these," she screamed.

When Nikki called her Mom later that night in hysterics, Krysta told her that she and Bill would agree to continue to pay for her education and that they had already made arrangements for Nikki to be able to live in the dorm even through the summer. Krysta told Nikki that she could stay in the hotel room we rented earlier so she wouldn't have to drive back to Pullman. Krysta made it clear that Nikki would not be welcome in their house until she could prove that she had learned her lesson about cheating.

Katelyn and I were married two weeks after the divorce from Nikki was final. We joined the swingers club with Bill and Krysta the weekend after our honeymoon. Kate and I had already made an agreement to allow some time each week for me to hang out with Abigale. Once we joined the swingers group, I attended one party each month with Abigale since she had no partner to bring. Kate insisted that it was okay because she would feel weird to attend the parties with her mother present.

It was nearly a year later that June showed up at one of the parties. She had recently married Gerry, one of the former members of the group that had lost his wife to breast cancer. They had met at a diner she was working at after divorcing Tom and distancing herself from her son Pete. Krysta had called to tell us that she would be there. When Gerry called to ask if June would be welcomed, Krysta had told them that she would be very welcome. It was not her fault that Tom had been a blackmailing pig.

Since all of the parties are recorded, June asked me if she could be my partner for the night. "I want to send a copy of the video to both of those pigs," she informed me. In order to protect the other guests, we used one of the back bedrooms. Gerry seemed ecstatic to be with my Katelyn for the night. June seemed to revel in being as nasty as she could while she sucked me off and then later had me fuck her in the rear. She made it a point to moan my name over and over and declare how wonderful my nine inch prick felt. I got a perverse pleasure out of knowing that Pete would see me fucking his Mother and his father would see it as well. When he gets out of prison.

--- END ---

Here is a sample from another story you may enjoy:

HOT EROTICA

HIRED FOR
Their Pleasure

A LATE BLOOMER'S 1ST TIME

JACK RYDER

"Mom was right, you have a gorgeous body," her voice startled me awake. I guess I must have stirred a bit when my body felt the pressure of someone sitting down on the bed next to me. I was still a bit groggy as I open my eyes to see Katie sitting there staring down at me. It took a few moments for to remember that I was completely naked. I instinctively reached to pull the blankets up but found that they had been kicked off onto the floor at some point in my sleep.

"Should I lock the door from now on, or is it acceptable for me to be naked every time you barge into my house unannounced?" My voice was hoarse and strained. I could see a look of lust on her face as she gawked at my flaccid prick. "You can be naked any time I come over," she told me with her eyes never leaving my dick. "Besides, Mom told you I would be over for breakfast." I glanced at the clock and it was ten after 9am.

"Do you think I'm pretty, Jake?" She whispered. "Oh hell yes, Katie...you are so very sexy," I told her as I felt a slight wiggle. Kathleen was wearing that tiny white bikini again. The way she was seated with one leg dangling off the bed and the other leg bent beside her, left her legs spread wide apart and I could see her pussy lips pressed tight against the crotch of her bottoms.

"But, I'm so skinny and I have no tits," she complained softly. "Even Stevie has bigger tits than I have," she lamented. "Are you kidding me?" I chuckled. "With that sexy slender body, those perky cone shaped tits are perfect." I gasped. "There are many men that prefer perky tits rather than the big globe type," I informed her. "You are incredibly sexy just the way you are, sweetie."

"Do you think you could like these as much as my mother's?" Katie reached up and untied her top so it fell forward to expose her breasts to me. "Ooooh Katie, look at you," I gasped as she reached back to undo the other string and her top fell off. Her small 32A cone shaped tits were less than a foot from my face. Her pink puffy nipples were exactly the same as her mother's but seemed more pronounced since her tits are more cone shaped. She also had those pure white triangles from her bikini tan line that has always aroused me deeply. "Damn, those are sexy," I gasped.

My dick had become fully rigid within seconds as I gazed at her exposed tits. "I see you're telling the truth," she giggled as she watched my dick bouncing against my belly. "You can touch them if you like," she whispered as she scooted a little closer and pulled her other leg up onto the bed. My hands were trembling noticeably as I reached forward to fondle both of her nubile little tits.

"That feels wonderful, Jake," she purred softly as she arched her back to press her breast firmly into my hands. I let go of her left breast and used placed my right hand around her waist so I could pull her forward. "Yes Jake, Yesssssss," she moaned as I wrapped my lips around her left puffy pink nipple and began to gently suck on it.

I felt her moving slightly and then felt her right hand wrapping around my rigid prick. "It's so big," she cooed when she saw that she could barely get her hand all the way around my girth. "Oooh, God Yes," I moaned as she started to gently stroke up and down my shaft. "So good, Jake, it feels s-o-o-o-o good," she gasped when I moved my mouth to suck on her other nipple.

My legs were quivering on the bed as she slowly jerked me off while I feasted on both of her perky tits. "I was so hard for you yesterday," I confessed as she got me closer and closer to orgasm. "You made my meat so wet when you were modeling those clothes," she answered me with a moan.

If you enjoyed this sample then look for **Hired For Their Pleasure.**

Also by this Author:

The Handyman Seduction

The Beer Bust Scandal

Scandalous Emotion

Intimate Relation

The Seduction of Kimi

Erotic Goes Hi-Tech

One at a Time

The Wizard Casey's Coven

The Inn Keeper's Wizard: When Love and Magic Collide

Trailer Trash Payback

Queer Intentions

Zoe's Fun House

Public Display

Test Drive

Breaking the Bonds

Trailer Trash Payback

The Hero's Welcome

The Twenty-Eight Day Cure

The Cougar Club

The Wife Swap

In Love with a Cougar

Stella for Christmas

The Long Ride Home

A Shot at Love

My Swedish Greta

The Second Honeymoon

Candy's Playmate

Sara's House of Hands

Loving My Sitter

His Wife and Her Husband

Bi-Curious Couple

Take Three, Mr. Writer

Hired For Their Pleasure

Blackmailed Nanny

The Daring Doppelgangers

Serving the Therapist

About the Author

Jack Ryder LOVES everything there is about sex!

When he is not involved with his "swinger" friends, enjoying a steamy threesome, or being part of a raunchy "gang bang", you can find him on first class planes, trains, and cruise ships. Traveling seems to be the BEST way to finding new and interesting sexmates for him. Sexmates. Plural. He lives with the saying "The More, The Merrier!"

He owns a successful business in New York. He writes as a hobby and also as sort of documentation of his mind-blowing sexcapades over the years. He is presently roaming around the streets of Manhattan but can be anywhere in the world too, since he travels often. So, beware! You just might be his next mate.

"The most fun thing I enjoy when writing my stories is trying to figure out which is fantasy and which was memory. ENJOY! (Preferably with a friend. *wink*) " -Jack Ryder-

From the Author

If you have any comments, suggestions, or would just like to get a little personal, please feel free to email me at:
jack_ryder@awesomeauthors.org

If you enjoyed any of my books then please share the love and click like on my books in Amazon.

If you write me a review and send me an email I will send you a free book, or many.
(Just know that these emails are filtered by my publisher.)

Good news is always welcome.

One Last Thing, For Kindle Readers...

When you turn the page, Kindle will give you the opportunity to rate this book and share your thoughts on Facebook and Twitter. If you enjoyed my writings, would you please take a few seconds to let your friends know about it? Because... when they enjoy they will be grateful to you and so will I.

Thank You!

Jack Ryder
jack_ryder@awesomeauthors.org